DREAM WITH ME NOW OF...
A DINOSAUR DASH

A CIP catalogue record for this title is available from the British Library.

ISBN 978 1 84963 662 9

www.austinmacauley.com

First Published (2015)
Austin Macauley Publishers Ltd.
25 Canada Square
Canary Wharf
London
E14 5LB

To Martin, Jay and Aiden

Thank you for believing in me.

About the Author

Born into a warm, loving, storytelling family Susan has always looked to give this wonderful experience to others. She has spent many years working with young children helping them to share her passion of writing and now, with the support of her own family, has set to making her dreams come true by passing on her world of imagination to children far and wide.

DREAM WITH ME NOW OF...
A DINOSAUR DASH

BY SUSAN CLIFFORD

ILLUSTRATED BY LUONG TRAN

Dream with me now of far off places, No need for luggage and no need for cases.

Just close your eyes and you will see, What's in store for you and me…

Let's go back to when dinosaurs roared

A scary journey, we won't be bore

We'll go back to a time when the mightiest ruled,

A time when dinosaurs fought and duelled.

A time of volcanoes and their spouting of rocks,

We'd better watch out so we don't get knocked.

The dinosaurs being such great big beasts,

Always on the look out for their next feast.

Let's hide in a cave, quick now let's hurry, And stay out the way so we've no need to worry.

Their big stomping feet and the swishing of tails,

The gnashing of teeth and their long sharp nails.

A snort of a breath, a loud piercing roar, That came from an angry dinosaur's jaw.

The ground began shaking as the beast walked by,

He had started his hunting with a watchful eye.

We've seen enough so let's not delay,

Let's hurry on back to our modern day.

Now open your eyes as wide as can be,
Think of the places we went to see,
All the fun things that we did today,
Now it's time for you to play.

Now close your eyes and go to sleep
And all our memories we'll keep,
The moon above now casts its beams
And so good night and pleasant
dreams.